SOPHOCLES'

ANTIGONE

The J. Paul Getty Museum
Los Angeles

My name is Teiresias—Teiresias the prophet. I need a staff to guide me on my way, and my day is no different from night, for I am blind.

But I possess a rare gift—I can see into the future. People call it a divine blessing. A blessing? At times it weighs on me like a curse. For although I can predict all that will happen, I do not have the power to change anything.

It is always these thoughts that fill me when I relate the story of Antigone. I saw her fate unfold before me, I knew what would happen—yet I was powerless to alter the terrible march of events. But hear her tale first, so that you may judge for yourself.

Antigone was the daughter of Oedipus, King of Thebes. Oedipus had another daughter, Ismene, and two sons, Eteocles and Polynices. When Oedipus died, his sons agreed to share the kingdom between them. They would rule over Thebes in turn, for one year each.

But after the first year had passed, Eteocles refused to give up the crown. Enraged by this, Polynices collected an army of seven princes and attacked Thebes. The seven princes died, each outside one of the seven gates of the city. Worse things were to follow.

The two brothers met in battle and killed each other. The crown then fell to their uncle, Creon.

Creon's task was a heavy one—to restore order to strife-torn Thebes. Already the city was full of murmurs—which of the princes had acted rightly? Eteocles' action had caused the war. Yet Polynices, whose claim was rightful, had led an alien army against his own city.

The morning Creon became king, I saw troubled times ahead for Thebes.

I was proved right.

Even before the sun had risen over Thebes, Antigone ran into her sister's chamber.

"Ismene! Terrible news! Our uncle Creon has declared Polynices a traitor who waged war against his own city. Eteocles has been named the true son of Thebes and is to be buried with ceremony."

"And ... what of Polynices?"

"Left for the vultures to eat. Our brother's body lies rotting outside the gates of the city, Ismene!"

"Unburied? Oh, poor Polynices!"

"Yes, Creon would have his soul wander the earth. And more! Whoever tries to bury Polynices will be put to death. Even you and I have lost our natural rights."

"What has possessed Creon? He has never been other than a loving uncle to us."

"But this he means in earnest. And we cannot allow it."

"But what can we do? We are mere women. We cannot defy Creon."

"And if we do?"

"Antigone, consider! Creon's order is the law."

"Do you feel nothing but fear? Would you ignore the laws of Heaven?"

"But we cannot bury him! You are mad!"

"I say we can. Now answer me directly Ismene: Will you go with me? He is my brother and yours—unless you disown him. I will not be a traitor to him."

"You judge me harshly Antigone! I do pity our dead brother. But if Creon has said he will not bury a traitor, he must mean it as a lesson to the people of Thebes. He is a just man."

"So you agree with him? Then do not pretend that you love our brother."

"Antigone! You speak in anger. I love Polynices as you do. But understand! Cities are ruled by the will of a king, not by the whims of women. If we bury Polynices, we will be named traitors too. They will drag us by our hair through the streets and put us to death!"

"Sometimes it is better not to think too much, as you do. Stay away, do as you please, I will not force you. I shall bury Polynices alone. I owe this deed to the brother I loved."

"Antigone, I plead with you. What is to be gained from such pride? There is nothing we can do but ask the dead to forgive us. There is no wisdom in going too far."

"Let this be your excuse then. But do not try to stop me."

Saying this, Antigone hurried away.

Ismene wept.

She mourned for her dead brother's soul, for she did love him. But equally, she wept for her headstrong young sister. Ismene could not fathom what moved her to such wild action. Antigone was soon to wed Creon's son Haemon—happiness lay before her. Why did she not know her limits? Why did she choose to defy the king of Thebes?

Ismene prayed that her sister would not carry out her dangerous plan.

I prayed too, for I could not bear the sacrifice of a young life. But what use was prayer? I could see Antigone was fixed in her resolve, hurrying that instant to her brother's corpse.

The cup was full, the water would overflow—she would bury Polynices. No law made by men would hold her back, for she had chosen to act by a natural law upheld by Heaven.

It is true, Heaven must have its own order—older and more eternal than the laws of men. Unburied, Polynices' spirit would be earthbound, condemned to haunt the city of Thebes forever. A sister could not abandon her brother to this fate. Antigone owed him this deed.

I saw all this, yet I prayed that she would change her mind.

But Antigone hurried on through the streets, intent on her fearful deed.

And even as she did so, Creon summoned the elders of Thebes to his palace. The city was full of murmurs—did Polynices deserve this terrible fate? Was he not a son of Thebes?

When the whispers reached his ears, Creon decided to address the elders, so that they, in turn, would persuade the citizens of Thebes of the wisdom of his rule.

"My friends, the two sons of Oedipus have killed each other, staining their hands with a brother's blood. The task of restoring justice to this kingdom falls to me, who was uncle to both princes.

"You all know my decree: Eteocles, who ruled this country and died fighting for it, will be honored with all the ceremony the brave deserve. But his brother Polynices, a traitor who led an alien army to attack the city of his fathers, shall be left unburied and unmourned. Sentries guard his body, and anyone who disobeys this law shall be put to death.

"Our country is a ship that bears us all, and fate has made me its captain. The ship has been seized by a storm and tossed by cruel waves. War has ripped her sails, sprung a hundred leaks in her hull, and I bear the burden of steering her to safety. I will steer clearly, with a firm hand.

"I would have it known that our country's enemy will never be our friend. So it is with Polynices, though he is my own nephew, tied to me by blood. For he has raised arms against his own people, and I count this no light matter. I place on you the duty of impressing my will upon the citizens of Thebes."

With this, Creon dismissed the elders, satisfied that they knew his hand was firm.

He did not know that his orders had already been defied.

Just as Creon rose, a guard ran into his chamber and fell, breathless, at his feet. Words tumbled out of him with none of the ceremony due to a king.

"I've run all the way from the gates sir! Of course, I did stop a couple of times to think if I should come at all. 'You're a fool to go looking for trouble!' I kept saying to myself. And finally I told myself, 'You'll pay for it in the end, either way. Best get on with it.' And then I did run sir, as fast as I could ..."

"Yes, yes, very good. What is the trouble?"

"I didn't do it sir! And I didn't see who did it either. It's not fair that I'm the one who has to get into trouble for it sir."

"Come, come, out with it."

"I'll tell you sir. But a man doesn't rush into trouble. I wanted to explain, that's all ..."

"Then speak up! Give me your news and be off."

"Alright sir, I'll tell you. It's the body. Someone buried it this morning sir. Not exactly buried sir, but covered it with a cloth."

"What! Who would dare to do such a thing?"

"I don't know sir! We saw nobody. Nothing. Whoever did it left no clue."

"Before I burst with rage, you fool, tell me, were you all asleep? Or have you sold yourself for money? Bribery is no new thing to this country."

"Oh, no sir! I don't know how it could have happened, sir. Me and two others, we had the early morning watch. It was almost light when the fog rolled in for a few minutes. Then when it blew away, we saw the body was covered. I swear by the gods in Heaven that none of us had a hand in it."

"How dare you burst in here to tell me this? You shall pay for this mistake with your life."

"Please forgive me sir. Don't punish me for my honesty. We drew lots to see who should come to you, and my luck was out—so it fell to me to bring you the news sir."

"You dare talk of luck to me? Unless you find the man who carried out this deed and bring him before me, you will be strung up from the city gates and left there to hang. Now go! Find the criminal who did this! We cannot have such men in Thebes."

The guard ran out of the palace, as breathless as when he had entered, thanking the gods that he had come away with his life.

But even as the guard hurried back to his post, terror returned to haunt him again—for his life was not his until he had found the man who had committed the dreadful deed.

An impossible task! To find a man nobody had seen.

But fear for his own life led the guard to forge a cunning plan. He and his comrades took away the cloth that covered Polynices' body, leaving it as if it had never been buried. Then they lay in wait, concealed in the bushes, hoping that the man would return and finish the task they had undone.

At midday, they were rewarded for their vigil. But they could not believe their eyes, for they saw ... not the man they were expecting, but a young woman.

The princess Antigone!

Cursing those who had laid Polynices' corpse bare, she covered it once more and performed her rites.

Of what use was my prayer for Antigone? She was reckless. She had buried Polynices once and by the grace of the gods escaped Creon's guards. Not content, she had come back to bury her brother a second time. No prayer could save her now. The guards seized her.

Calm and unafraid, prepared to meet her fate, she walked with them to Creon's palace.

When Creon saw who the guards dragged before him, he was overcome with horror.

"You fools! Have you taken leave of your senses? Do you know who she is? Release her at once! Leave us, be off! ... Now, how did you come into the hands of these men, child?"

"They seized me as I buried Polynices."

"Antigone! What is this!"

"The truth."

"What!"

"Yes! Why do you start? There is nothing shameful in honoring a dead brother."

"You buried Polynices!"

"Yes, I did."

"And ... you were aware that I had forbidden it?"

"I knew. All of Thebes knew."

"And yet you dared disobey my law? Why?"

"The gods did not make that law, and I was not afraid of a law made by a man."

"Indeed! And by honoring the brother who was a traitor, you chose to insult the other."

"Burying the dead is an insult to no one."

"Traitors and heroes cannot be treated as equal."

"Would the gods consider one a traitor and the other a hero? Did not Eteocles begin the war by refusing to give Polynices his right to the kingdom?"

"Yes, Eteocles was unjust toward his brother, but Polynices rose against his own country. Can you not see whose crime is greater?"

"I honored no criminal, but only did my duty by the brother I loved."

"I tire of this talk! Do you know the penalty for your deed? It is death."

"We all must die sometime. And if I am to die saving my brother's soul, then that is my fate. But save him I must. And I prefer to die than to live with the knowledge that I let my brother's corpse be thrown to the vultures."

"Antigone, you are the daughter of King Oedipus. Yours is the duty of upholding the law of the land, not defying it. Or tell me, did you think that as my niece you could escape punishment?"

"Even if I had been a poor maid, I would have done the same."

"But you are not a maid, you are a princess. Act as a princess should. Do you think that I had no grief in my heart for Polynices? I had to harden it so that I could act rightly as a king.

Polynices was a traitor to Thebes, and it is as the ruler of Thebes that I sentenced him to this fate."

"And it is as his sister that I save him from it. Now we have both done our duties."

"Take care what you say, Antigone. Do you compare your childish act with that of a ruler of men?"

"I do not count my duty as any less than yours. I know that what I did is right, though you may call it childish. But kings are fortunate. They can decide what is right and wrong."

"You do not make it easy for me, Antigone. You are headstrong. But let me be lenient toward your insolence and call it merely foolish talk. Remember it is the trees that do not bend with the wind that are easily snapped!"

"Then do with me as you will. I will not bend."

"Do not taunt me, Antigone. You were always an impudent girl, but now you go too far. Would I have given so much ear to anyone else who had committed this crime? I would have them put to death instantly. You are of my blood, closer to me than anyone but my own son. Now listen carefully. I do not want to put you to death for a foolish mistake. You are to marry my son Haemon, your life is before you. Do not waste it. Now, did you tell anyone else of this deed?"

"Why do you ask? Only Ismene, my sister."

"You are certain of this?"

"Yes! But she had no hand in it."

"I did not think so. She has more wisdom than you do."

"The courageous would not consider it wisdom."

"You try my patience dearly, Antigone. But it is an uncle's duty to protect his niece. Now, do as I say. Return to your chamber and do not breathe a word of this to anyone. I have ways to silence the guards—this should not reach the ears of the people. We will put this matter to rest. You will have your life, but first swear this: You will not try to bury Polynices again."

"You think you can give my life to me as you would give a child a toy? My act is not a foolish whim—I stand by it. I do not want to be spared. Now do with me as you think right."

"You little fool! Do you mock me? I have put aside my duty as a king to act as an uncle should towards a niece he loved ..."

"And your niece's duty to her brother? What of that?"

"Mad woman! Enough! I will not waste my words on your deaf ears any longer. Nothing can save you."

"And now that you have condemned me, what will you do? Kill me? I am prepared for it."

"You leave me no choice! You are unrepentant! Gods, I have nurtured a viper who now turns to strike me! No woman shall rule me as long as I live. If I let this crime go unpunished, she will have had the power of a king, and I the weakness of a woman. No, Antigone! You will not escape the consequence of your insolence."

"I never thought so. Do what you must. I have done what I should."

"If you are determined to die, then die! Go join your brother in the world below. Guards! Take her away!"

The die was cast. Antigone's fate was sealed. I wondered if it could have been otherwise. Could she have spoken with a tongue less rough? Bent a little, pleaded her case with craftier words? Then, perhaps, Creon would not have condemned her.

But if she had acted so, she would not be Antigone—strong in her beliefs, reckless, knowing no fear. True to her nature, she had challenged Creon in a manner no one dared. She had denied him any power over her—as king or as uncle. By this, she sealed her fate.

And Creon? Could he not have seen Antigone as she was—a strong-willed woman with convictions as powerful as his? Had he done so, Antigone might have reasoned with him differently.

But had he done so, he would not be Creon—a proud, just man. Proud men stand alone, seeing no conviction other than their own. And did he not consider defiance all the more impertinent coming from a woman?

No, an encounter between Antigone and Creon could not have been otherwise.

This I knew, yet I prayed in the name of the house of Oedipus for it all to be undone.

And with the same prayer on his lips, Prince Haemon hastened to his father to reason with him.

"Father! What is the news that sounds through Thebes!"

"It is true, Haemon. Your bride has been sentenced to death, and with reason. So, have you come to berate your father, or do you stand by his side?"

"Do not doubt my loyalty."

"Good. A father's greatest strength is a loyal son who strikes his enemies and embraces his friends."

"You confuse me! Do you call Antigone our enemy? My bride, your own niece?"

"Haemon! Do not think my decision was a light one. Antigone was unrepentant. She left me no choice. I cannot demand obedience from my subjects when I breed rebellion under my own roof. I will not have it said that Creon was conquered by a lawless woman."

"Lawless? Antigone is strong willed, but just in her reasoning."

"Do not abandon your own reason for a passing fancy. Is this the bride you would wish for yourself?"

"I could not ask for a better one. I only beg you to see that yours is not the only view. I have heard whispers of pity for Antigone, condemned for a courageous deed. What was her crime? To save a dead brother's soul by honoring the wishes of the gods!"

"Shame! You, my own son, repeat such slanderous treason to me? Would you take the side of a woman against me?"

"For your own good, father. Do you wish to speak only and hear not a word in reply? People do not dare to oppose you, for you wield your power with a heavy hand. I see no disgrace for even the wisest of men to take counsel from other people."

"And your counsel is that I should honor a lawbreaker!"

"The people of Thebes do not think her one."

"You want the people to rule me? It is for the king to decide what is best for Thebes."

"Father, a city is no city if it is ruled by one man's law."

"Now I see your purpose! I thought your loyalty was to me, but you have come here only to uphold a woman against your own father!"

"Only because you make a grave mistake. Intent upon your own laws, you have forgotten to give respect to the gods."

"You dare talk to me like this? You shall never marry her. She dies this very evening."

"If she dies, her death will cause another death."

"Would you threaten me, you woman's slave?"

Terrible words to pass between a father and his son! Even as Haemon left the palace, Creon gave orders for Antigone to be walled up alive in a cave outside the city, and left to die.

Creon had lost all his powers of reason—flung into the sea of his own pride. Caught in that dark tide, he took Haemon's parting words as a threat to himself. Had he known what Haemon meant, Creon might well have checked his anger.

But the swirl of tragedy spared no one. Antigone lay in a dark cave, left to her cruel fate. Haemon stumbled through the city to her side, holding a frayed thread of hope that he could save her yet. And Creon sat bowed, with eyes as blind as mine ...

I could bear it any more. I had foreseen these events but had prayed that they would not come to pass. What could I possibly do now, when the last threads were unraveling themselves? Yet I could not stand aside and let the tragedy flow on, raising no hand to avert it.

I decided to use the powers of my art and undertake a sacrifice to appease the gods.

But my sacrifice produced omens so grim and fearful that I went at once to Creon.

"Creon, I wish to speak with you—a matter most urgent."

"Aged Teiresias, is it news you bring? I am weary and my ear can hold no more."

"You would do well to mark my words, for I bring no ordinary tidings. Before I came to you, I made an offering to the gods. Several times I made to light the sacrificial fire, but no flame rose up. I say that the gods are angry—they do not accept our sacrifices because Thebes is tainted through your folly. Think on your actions, for it is you who have displeased the gods."

"Begone, old man! Have you come to rail against me too? Have I not had enough thrown at my ears already? Even the wisest and most respected of men takes the side of traitors and rebels! Is it for me alone to steer this country straight?"

"Creon! You speak rashly. You know that it is through my counsel that you have kept this kingdom safe. Is there a man who has not made a mistake? Give up your stubborn will and correct your folly. Give the dead Polynices his right. Do you consider it bravery to stab a dead man?"

"Enough! I will not hear this again! Have you been bribed by the friends of Polynices that you plead thus?"

"Arrogant, unbridled tongue! Have you the power of a god? I will not spare you the terrible truth. Mark my prophesy well. Before the sun sets, your own son will die. A corpse for a corpse. Your palace will echo with your own solitary wails. Already the fathers of the seven princes you have left unburied are thirsting for your blood. With this knowledge I leave you. I did not wish to aim so many barbs at your heart, but you have provoked me."

The force of my outburst shook Creon's resolve.

In all the years that his hair had turned from dark to silver, my prophesies had never failed him. He was gripped with terror at what I had said, for the first time floundering in his convictions. On the one hand, his pride would not allow him to yield. Equally, he could not abide by his decision and bring ruin upon his own head.

In the end, terror won over pride. Creon reversed his will.

He ordered his servants to bury Polynices and his allies, the seven princes, with all the rites that Heaven demanded. Then, gathering his guards together, he hastened to the cave where Antigone was kept, to break down the rocky walls that sealed her.

But Creon reached the cave too late. The walls were already broken.

And he saw ... Oh, most terrible sight!

At the far end of the cave was Antigone—hanging from a noose of linen. Haemon lay at her feet, stabbed in the heart with his own sword. Seeing that his love had killed herself, he had taken his own life.

Broken by sorrow, Creon asked to be led out of the cave, taking the hand of his guard like a child.

I had foretold this, yet I could not help but grieve for Creon, humbled so mercilessly by the gods. Once a king to be envied, he had, with his own power, brought destruction upon his head. My prophecy, alas, had come true.

And so I come to the end of my tragic tale, filled with pity for the dead—and for the living.

There is no more to tell, yet the story of Antigone does not end in my mind.

I wonder what moves me, time and again, to tell this tale of courage and sorrow. Perhaps the hope that those who hear it may contemplate, as I do, the actions of human beings.

Caught in my own fear, I had witnessed the drama unfold, praying that Antigone should not pay too dear a price for her beliefs. Now, when my tale is done and my grief has subsided, the events shape themselves anew before me. I reflect once more on her fate, and I begin to wonder.

Perhaps Antigone's death was not wholly in vain. For holding steadfast to her beliefs, did she not question powers far greater than herself? And in going to her death unafraid, she bore the consequences of her actions willingly. Is this not a triumph of freedom?

These thoughts I leave for those who hear my tale to ponder.

GREEK THEATER

This story was inspired by the Greek play *Antigone*, written by Sophocles in the fifth century B.C. It won the first prize at the annual drama festival held in the city of Athens in ancient Greece.

Such contests were common at that time. The ancient Greeks enjoyed drama and spectacle, staged in magnificent theaters scooped out of hillsides. Often the entire town gathered to watch the plays, and free tickets were given to those who could not afford to buy them. Comedy and tragedy played alternately in these theaters.

Greek tragedies dealt with themes of fate, individual conscience, the conflict between good and evil, and human suffering. The heroes and heroines of tragedies were from royal families—kings and queens, who experienced some kind of conflict. The struggle with their own conscience often destroyed the hero or heroine, and those involved with them.

A tragedy was expected to evoke feelings of dread, horror, and pain in the viewers—emotions that were released by watching the play to its final conclusion. The viewer then understood and felt strengthened by the noble meanings of tragedy—the struggle of the individual against powerful forces.

Sophocles' Antigone

First published in English by the J. Paul Getty Museum
1200 Getty Center Drive, Suite 1000
Los Angeles, California 90049-1687

At the J. Paul Getty Museum:
Christopher Hudson, Publisher
Mark Greenberg, Managing Editor

At Tara Publishing:
Rathna Ramanathan, Designer
C. Arumugam, Production Coordinator

Library of Congress Card Number: 2001086941

ISBN: 0-89236-637-0

Printed and bound in India